TOO MANY PUPPIES

PUPPIES

By Lisa Trusiani Parker

Illustrated by S. I. Artists

A GOLDEN BOOK • NEW YORK

Golden Books Publishing Company, Inc., Racine, Wisconsin 53404

Dear Barbie,

My dog just had five puppies. They're really cute.

I want to keep them all, but my mom says each puppy needs a home of its own. I'm only allowed to keep one and I have to give the rest away.

What should I do, Barbie?

Love,
Donna

$\mathcal{B}$arbie sat down to answer Donna's letter. She wrote:

Dear Donna,
    Your question reminds me of the time my friend
Sara's dog, Sheba, had puppies. Sara loved the puppies
and wanted to keep them all, too.

Barbie continued her letter to Donna. And this is the
story she told. . . .

Barbie and Sara were getting ready to meet Ken at the
roller rink. "Hurry, Sara," called Barbie, "or we'll be late."
"I'm ready, but I can't find my helmet," Sara said.

Just then Sheba came in, dragging the helmet. "She's just into *everything* lately," Sara said. "I wonder why she's acting like this."

"Sheba's looking for a good place to have her puppies," Barbie said.

"Look," Sara said. "Sheba's found a spot under the piano."
"Let's try to make her comfortable," Barbie suggested.

The next morning, Sara called Barbie. "I have a surprise for you," Sara said.

When Barbie got to Sara's house, she didn't find one surprise—she found six!

Soon Ken and Skipper arrived. "How cute!" Skipper cried.
"But how will you take care of six puppies?" Ken asked.
"I think I can handle them," said Sara.
"I'll help you," Barbie promised.

Barbie visited Sara often to help with the puppies. One day while the puppies were napping, the two friends took Sheba out for a walk, and then stopped for some pizza.

"Thanks so much for all your help," Sara said.
"I've enjoyed it," Barbie said. "Soon I'll be helping with
the BE KIND TO ANIMALS FESTIVAL at the Community Center."
"I'd help, too," Sara said. "But I'm so busy right now."

Sara got busier every day. Soon the puppies were eating one another's food! To be sure that they were all getting enough, Barbie and Sara took turns watching them eat.

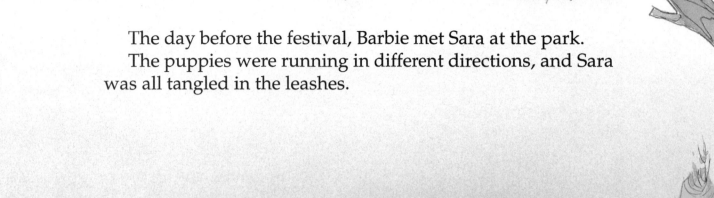

The day before the festival, Barbie met Sara at the park.
The puppies were running in different directions, and Sara
was all tangled in the leashes.

After Barbie untangled the leashes, she talked to Sara about finding good homes for the puppies. "Each one will be able to get so much more attention," Barbie explained.

"Oh, I could never give them away," Sara said.

Suddenly Barbie remembered her meeting with Mrs. Olsen, the festival organizer. Barbie asked Sara to come along. They rounded up the puppies and walked to the Community Center.

"Hi!" called Mrs. Olsen. "Let's walk over to the festival site. It's right across the park."

"All right," Barbie said. "But can we leave the puppies in the yard?" Mrs. Olsen agreed to let them stay.

But the frisky puppies managed to crawl under the fence and head for the park.

All the children tried to catch the runaway pups.

Barbie heard the commotion and knew she had to act fast.
"Hurry," she called to Sara and Mrs. Olsen.
Soon all the puppies were rounded up.

They brought the puppies back to the center. "Each puppy has a fun playmate," said Mrs. Olsen.

Barbie and Sara listened to a little girl tell one of the puppies: "I'm Melinda, and I think I'll call you Muffy."

"You're right," Sara told Barbie. "I really can't give the pups all the attention they need."

"I have an idea," said Barbie. "Meet me at the festival tomorrow morning at eight o'clock—and bring the puppies."

When Sara arrived at the festival, she saw that Barbie had
set up an Adopt a Puppy booth. "Great idea!" said Sara.
Soon Melinda arrived with her parents and asked to adopt
Muffy.

Before long, four more pups were adopted. They all went to people that Sara believed would provide very good homes. Sara kept the last puppy for herself.

"Thanks, Barbie," said Sara. "I don't know what I would have done without you."

Barbie smiled as she finished her letter to Donna:

The best thing you can do now is to pick a puppy for yourself. Start talking to friends about the other puppies. Then you'll know that each puppy is going to a safe, caring home. Best of all, the one you keep will get all your love.

Love,

Barbie